12/200

D0597702

Library of Congress Cataloging-in-Publication Data Available.

ISBN 0-439-08206-4

10 9 8 7 6 5 4 3 2 1   9/9 0/0 01 02 03

Printed in France
First American edition, October 1999

The Perfume of Memory

by MICHELLE NIKLY
illustrated by JEAN CLAVERIE

ARTHUR A. LEVINE BOOKS
AN IMPRINT OF SCHOLASTIC PRESS

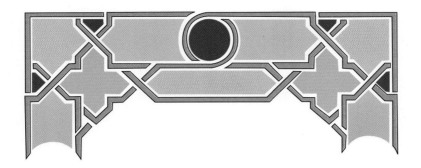

*E*VERYONE KNOWS THAT
a wonderful scent is a breath away from a memory.

But in a faraway land, long, long ago, there was
a place where people forgot this power. Which was
strange, considering the kind of place it was. For
there, every sunrise had its own subtle fragrance,
blowing off the graceful palms and the slowly
baking sands, rising from the golden bricks of the
roads and walls. Sometimes it seemed as if even the
rays of the sun itself gave off the scent of happiness,
or serenity.

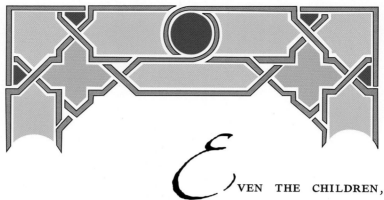

VEN THE CHILDREN,
running home from school with aromatic packages
clutched in their hands, smelled like powder and
fresh mud and grass clippings.

You see, at one time in this special place, every
child—boy or girl, big or small—was given the
chance to study the mysterious art of perfume
making. For it was everyone's dream to become the
Royal Perfume Maker.

But that was long before our story begins, alas.
For one day a little girl, rushing to school, spilled
essence of skunk on the Royal Advisor. The angry
fellow declared that only boys should be allowed to
be perfume makers. And before long people forgot
that it had ever been different.

And that was only the beginning of a forgetfulness that swept the country. People forgot perfume
formulas, of course. But they also forgot each other's
birthdays, and they forgot the endings of songs.
They remembered laws, like the Royal Advisor's,
but they forgot how to think for themselves. They
forgot their own history.

And when the King sent the Royal Advisor to a
foreign land to get advice about the problem, his
guide forgot the way back, and the party was lost.
And before long the people forgot all about the
Royal Advisor himself.

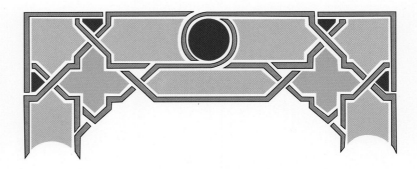

OW IN ONE PART OF
the land there lived a kindly perfume maker named
Ahmad and his daughter, Yasmin.

Yasmin's mother, for whom she was named, had
died in giving birth, and ever since Ahmad had been
finding ways to keep her memory alive.

"Smell this," he would tell Yasmin, showing her
a vial that held the essence of mint and wind. "This
makes me think of your mother on a cool spring day."

Yasmin would smile and almost think she
remembered, even though she couldn't—she'd been
too young, of course. But she watched everything
her father did, taking notes, studying potions. And
soon enough she started making perfumes of her
own.

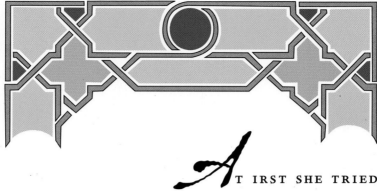

AT IRST SHE TRIED
to do exactly as her father had done, following
his formulas as closely as possible.

"Yes. Good," he'd say. "You've captured the smell
of the freshest sea breeze. . . ." Other times he'd
simply place his nose over the vial Yasmin had
handed him, take a delicate sniff, and close his
eyes, smiling to himself. "Wonderful, Yasmin.
Marvelous."

But one day she brought her father something
totally different. Something she'd made without
formulas or guidance. A perfume that came from
everything she knew about her mother, about her
father . . . and about herself. She handed it to
Ahmad with trembling hands.

Ahmad sniffed the perfume cautiously. Then he
closed his eyes, but Yasmin could not tell what he
was thinking.

"Yasmin," he said at last, "this is nothing like
what I've taught you." He paused as Yasmin felt the
beginnings of disappointment. "But it is the best
you've ever created. Because it is totally original.
Playful. Roguish. It makes me feel free of care. Your
mother would be proud." And then he took her in
his arms and held her tightly. "We must enter this
perfume in the Great Contest!"

"Yes!" cried Yasmin.

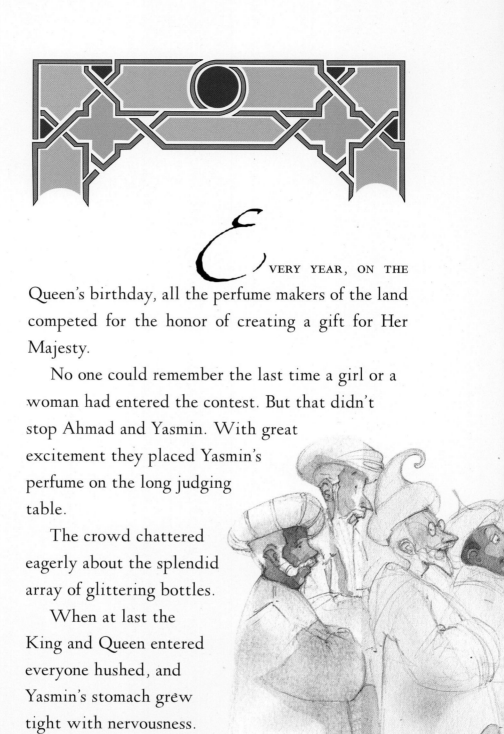

$\mathcal{E}$VERY YEAR, ON THE Queen's birthday, all the perfume makers of the land competed for the honor of creating a gift for Her Majesty.

No one could remember the last time a girl or a woman had entered the contest. But that didn't stop Ahmad and Yasmin. With great excitement they placed Yasmin's perfume on the long judging table.

The crowd chattered eagerly about the splendid array of glittering bottles.

When at last the King and Queen entered everyone hushed, and Yasmin's stomach grew tight with nervousness. What would happen if her perfume— a girl's perfume— were chosen?

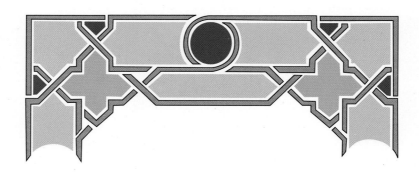

At last the
judging began. As the fragrances reached the
audience, the crowd murmured its approval. The
Queen first opened a round flask with a musky,
heavy smell. Then she opened a long, skinny
flask that contained a fragrance so faint
it could almost have been water.
After each one the Queen would
turn and smile graciously at the
audience.

Yasmin thought the Queen was
the most elegant and graceful
person she had ever seen—exactly
as she imagined her mother
must have been. Yasmin
pictured the Queen choosing
her flask and saying, "This scent
is as good as any man's. Better."

And then the Queen did
reach for Yasmin's perfume.
But her fingers hesitated. . . .
She was drawn to the one
other bottle remaining.

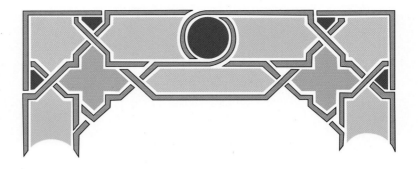

*T*HE QUEEN REMOVED the sinuously curved stopper. Tentatively she waved it in the air before her face, not yet ready to bring it all the way to her nose.

For this perfume had nothing in common with the ones before it. It was dark, velvety, seductive, . . . like the first soft touch of a pillow at the start of a deep, deep sleep.

As the first waves of the scent reached the audience, they sighed all together: a sound of delighted appreciation, but soft, like a lullaby. Only Yasmin turned to her father and said with conviction, "That perfume is dangerous. The Queen mustn't choose it! She mustn't!"

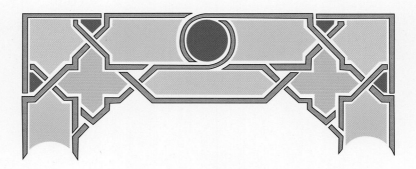

UT THE QUEEN had already made her choice. "This perfume receives the first prize," she announced. She called for the perfume's creator, and a man stepped forward, his face half-hidden under a large hood.

In the time-honored tradition of the country, the man kneeled before the Queen as she smiled and acknowledged him. "Please tell me the name of your perfume," she said, delicately applying a drop to each side of her neck.

But before the man could answer, the Queen became faint. Her knees buckled and she fell to the floor. Her servants and advisors and the people in the audience crowded around to help her, but the hooded man called out, "I have named this perfume Forgetfulness. Because I will never forget the wrongs done me by this Queen and her people. I was once the Royal Advisor. . . ." At this the crowd gasped, recognizing him at last. "Did anyone help me when I was lost? Did anyone remember my great deeds for this country? Well, perhaps you'll remember me now!" And before anyone could stop him, he disappeared from the room.

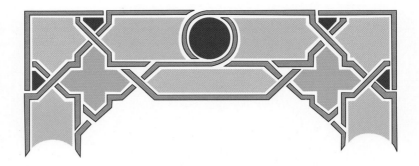

$\mathcal{S}$OON AFTER, THE QUEEN awoke, but she was completely changed. Gone were her memories of growing up, of becoming Queen, of ruling the country. She had completely forgotten who she was.

The King was no comfort to her, for she didn't recognize him. She woke in the night, calling for her nanny or her mother. All that would soothe her was a doll she'd had as a girl.

Desperate, the King promised that anyone who could cure his wife would have his greatest wish fulfilled. But Yasmin wasn't thinking of a reward; she already had an idea of how to help.

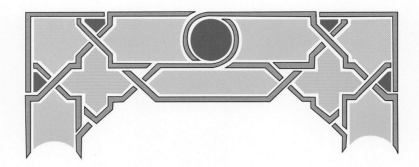

SOON YASMIN AND AHMAD
were given an audience with the Queen. They
entered the courtyard with lacquered boxes filled
with clinking glass. The Royal Physician was
dubious. "How can he help?" he scoffed. "He's no
doctor!"

But Ahmad said, "It's my daughter who will
help. Watch."

Then, slowly and gently, Yasmin began pulling
out vials and placing them on a golden tray before
the Queen. One by one she uncorked the flasks and
introduced each scent.

"Smell the white bloom of the Casablanca lily,
which grew on the walls of your parents' house.
Remember?" And the Queen remembered.

"This is the oil of myrrh and eucalyptus that was
placed on your head when you were anointed
Queen. Remember?" And the Queen remembered.

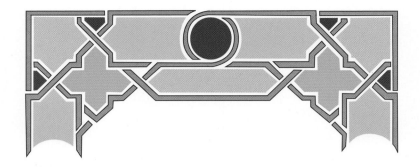

MEMORY BY MEMORY,
Yasmin brought the Queen to herself. Still, she
hesitated before opening the final flask. Should she
bring back all of the Queen's memories? What
would happen if the Queen remembered that girls
were forbidden to be perfume makers?

But Yasmin knew what she must do. And so she
opened the flask that smelled of parchment and of
ink, of rules and laws that the Queen had signed and
the King had sealed as they reigned together.

The Queen rose to her feet and beckoned for
Ahmad and Yasmin to follow her. Together they
went to the courtyard where the King paced back
and forth. When the King and Queen saw each
other, they both cried out and ran into each other's
arms.

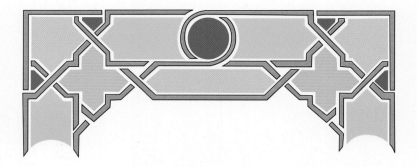

*F*IRST THE KING AND Queen made a new law that anyone who was talented enough could become the Royal Perfume Maker. As clearly, Yasmin was.

Then the King remembered his promise to grant Ahmad and Yasmin a wish. Ahmad asked to plant Jasmine bushes throughout the kingdom, so the air would smell always of summer.

And Yasmin? She asked that a Royal Storyteller be appointed, so no one would ever again forget the proud history of the land and the people who lived there. And she asked that the new position be given to the Royal Advisor, who needed something to do while in jail.

The first thing he wrote down was this story.